Bella
dancerella™

The Cinderella Wand

7

Written by
Poppy Rose

ABC
Books

Illustrated by
Omar Aranda

It was a cold, bleak day and rain poured from
the farmhouse eaves like a tap. 'Aren't you glad
you're helping me look for the key that unlocks the
drawers of Mum's jewellery box and not out there,
rounding sheep, Roy?' Bella asked.

'It's rained every day since we got home from Paris,'
Roy woofed. 'And it hasn't snowed inside the jewellery
box since Christmas Eve. In fact, there's been no sign
of magic at all! I think we were both overtired that
night and just imagined it. It was midnight after all.'

'We did not imagine it!' Bella protested. 'It did happen and when we find the key, we will see magic happen again. I know it!'

'We've looked everywhere,' Roy woofed.

'Hey, you two,' Dad said, opening the attic door. 'We'll need to leave at twelve-thirty for your State Ballet Company try-outs, okay?'

Bella glanced at the clock. 'We'll be down soon. I'm super-excited about these try-outs. There's no way I want to be late!'

'See you soon then,' Dad said, closing the door behind him.

Just then, a golden ray of sunlight broke through the clouds and shone in the window. Bella watched, mesmerised, as tiny dust particles danced, caught in a dazzle of light.

And then she saw it.

'**Roy, look!**' Bella exclaimed, pointing. '**It's the key!**'

'But what if the drawers are empty?' woofed Roy gently.

'Then we'll know once and for all,' Bella whispered,
turning the key.

Two drawers sprang open. Bella looked inside the first
one. 'It's a bracelet with a ballerina padlock,' she said.

'And what's in the other drawer?' woofed Roy.

'Just the shape of a tiny wand cut into some foam —
and the other drawers are still locked,' Bella mumbled,
shoulders slumping.

'Well, try on your mum's bracelet,' woofed Roy.

Bella laid the bracelet over her wrist and closed the clasp.

All at once, the mirror shook. Bright light sprang
from the bracelet. The light swirled and twisted.
It began disappearing into the mirror, and it lifted
Bella and Roy with it.

And in the blink of an eye they had vanished
through the mirror.

Bella shook herself and sat upright. 'Where are we, Roy? And where are we going?' she asked.

'You're in Tututopia of course,' squeaked a white mouse sitting opposite them. 'And on your way to the Kingdom of Fairy Godmothers.'

'But I should be at home! I'll be late for my ballet try-outs,' Bella said, looking startled.

Roy peered at the signpost. 'There's a fairy godmother for pets,' he woofed, his tail wagging.

'Listen to me,' squeaked the mouse. 'Cinderella's fairy godmother needs your help urgently. And you will **fix** this mess, won't you?'

'Fix what mess?' Bella asked as the coach came to a stop.

The mouse hopped from the carriage and held the door open. 'You'll find out,' he snapped.

'It's the **fairy** godmother's **palace!**' Roy woofed, springing from the carriage. 'Come on, Bella! You wanted magic,* and now the fairy godmother needs your help.'

As Bella stared at the huge, daunting palace, its large double doors flew open. The fairy godmother stepped out, smiled and waved at Bella.

Bella **leapt** from the carriage and ran up the drive.

Once inside, the fairy godmother's eyes swept over the little group. 'How lovely that you've come,' she said to Bella. 'But you look a bit young to be Cinderella for opening night. Of course, opening night will be a disaster now and it's all my fault.'

'Oh, I'm not Cinderella, I'm ...'

'And you are to be the coachman, I suppose,' the fairy godmother continued, giving Roy a look. **_'Goodness me!'_**

Bella and Roy exchanged a quick glance.

'And I can't turn the mice into horses,' she then told the mouse. **_'AND_** we'll be having lots of pumpkin soup for dinner instead of a carriage. Obviously!'

'Why can't you do all that?' Bella asked. 'That's what you do for Cinderella, isn't it?'

'Yes, of course it is,' the fairy godmother answered, walking Bella to a wooden cabinet. 'But I can only do it with my Cinderella wand and it has been stolen, as you can see.'

'Then you must get it back quickly!' Bella cried.

'Yes, *you* simply must,' the fairy godmother agreed, taking two other wands from the cabinet.

'Me!' Bella exclaimed. 'I'm really sorry but I can't possibly. You see, I have important ballet try-outs and …'

'The ballet is due to open at the Vienna State Opera House very soon and unless you can get that wand back, there will be no ball gown, no horses and carriage and no glass slippers!' the fairy godmother said, dismissing Bella's protests. 'Now, gather round my seeing fountain and I'll show you what happened to the wand.'

'You know what happened to it?' Bella asked, suddenly curious.

'Of course,' answered the fairy godmother, dragging the seeing wand through the fountain water. She blew gently into the wand and two bubbles floated before them. Bella, Roy and the mouse watched as the bubbles filled with visions of Cinderella's *evil* stepsisters with the wand.

'My travelling spell will take you to the *evil* stepsisters' house,' the fairy godmother said, giving Bella an hourglass. 'When all the sand has fallen through this hourglass, my spell will wear off and you'll be transported in an instant. With or without the Cinderella wand.'

'Where is the house of the *evil* stepsisters?' woofed Roy.

'In the Kingdom of *Evil* Characters,' the fairy godmother replied, raising her travel wand. 'Be very, very careful there. Don't stray.'

The fairy godmother cast her spell, and Bella, Roy and the mouse were gone.

'We're in the *evil* stepsisters' kitchen,' Bella whispered,
eyes wide.

'Yes!' woofed Roy. 'And it's a mess. No Cinderella
cleaning for them.'

'Up the stairs,' the mouse whispered. 'The wand was
on the *evil* stepsisters' pillow.'

But as they began creeping slowly up the stairs,
a cackle of laughter broke the silence.

'**Oh no!**' Bella said. 'They're out on the terrace and heading this way!'

'They'll catch us for sure,' squeaked the mouse.

'Stay against the wall,' Bella urged, her heart pounding. 'Be as still as a mouse, my little mouse.'

They all pressed themselves quietly against the wall.

23

The *evil* stepsisters headed straight for the kitchen and helped themselves to cackle cake and bitter berry juice.

Bella let out her breath and stole a quick look at them from behind. 'The wand's in her hair,' she whispered. 'It's holding up her bun.'

'How are we going to get it from there without her knowing?' squeaked the mouse, beginning to tremble.

'Don't worry, we'll think of something,' woofed Roy, crouching down. 'Climb on and grab hold of my collar, little mouse. You'll be safer there.'

The three watched silently as the sisters picked up their cake and drinks and turned to go back to the terrace.

Once they'd left, the group crept over to the doors and peeked through the glass.

'They look so scary and mean,' Bella whispered, handing the hourglass to the mouse.

'They're cruel and nasty,' squeaked the mouse. 'And the cackle cake and bitter berry juice keep them that way.'

'Look,' Bella whispered. 'She's taken the wand from her hair and put it on the table.'

'That makes things a bit easier,' woofed Roy.

'The sand is falling fast through the hourglass, though,' squeaked the mouse. **'We're running out of time!'**

'I'll quickly snatch it,' Bella said, determined. 'Then we'll make a run for it.'

Bella gingerly opened the door. SQQQQUUUUUUEAK went the hinges and Bella let out a gasp.

'Shut the door,' the *evil* stepsister grumbled between sips of bitter berry juice.

'You shut it,' the other mumbled through mouthfuls of cackle cake.

Bella breathed more easily when neither sister moved. Then she snuck up behind them, moving towards the wand.

As Bella reached for the wand,
a bony hand picked it up.

The hand waved it around and then dropped it in her cup.

Bella tried once again, but the cup fell over.

The wand flew from the table and landed in the clover.

The sisters spun round, but Bella moved fast.

She raced to the wand and she had it at last.

But when she turned back, she saw they had Roy.

They were pulling on his ears
as though he were a toy.

'Let him go!' Bella cried. 'Then I'll give you the wand.'
'We'll take that wand and deal with you later,' snarled
one of the *evil* stepsisters.

The mouse was dangling silently from Roy's collar.
He caught Bella's eye and pointed to the hourglass.
Suddenly, Bella knew exactly what she had to do.

Bella waited until the last few grains of sand began falling through the hourglass, then she lunged forwards and grabbed onto Roy's collar. 'To the Vienna State Opera House we go!' she cried.

As the last grain of sand fell, all three vanished, leaving two bewildered sisters behind.

As the carriage pulled up outside the Opera House, a light dusting of snow began to softly fall.

'Austria is so beautiful at this time of year, but there's no time to waste,' the fairy godmother said. 'We must get you on stage!'

'But I can't possibly be Cinderella in the big scene,' Bella babbled, racing to keep up. 'I don't even know how to dance the part.'

'But of course you can and you will,' the fairy godmother urged, stifling a giggle. 'Once you're in the magic slippers, you'll know every step by heart forever. You certainly did a good job getting my wand back, but you don't know much about magic, do you?'

'And what about my ballet try-outs?' Bella asked. 'I've missed them by now, anyway, I suppose.'

Before Bella could say anything else, she found herself centre stage as Cinderella. Every velvet seat and opera box in the grand theatre was filled with people.

Bella watched in awe as the fairy godmother turned the pumpkin into a carriage. She laughed as she saw her little mouse friend transformed into a horse and Roy transformed from her loyal dog to the coachman.

Next, the fairy godmother took Bella's hand. She spun her round and round, waving her wand as she did.

Bella looked at her ball gown, stunned. Then she peered out at the audience as the orchestra began to play.

The magic slippers led her and Bella danced the scene perfectly to the end.

As the curtains closed on the stage, the fairy godmother waved her wand once more. Back came Roy, the pumpkin and mice. Gone was the dress and the glimmering jewels.

'That was **THE BEST**!' Bella exclaimed, eyes shining bright. 'To dance like that in this amazing theatre, in front of all those people! I still can't believe I did it!'

'You'll always be able to perform that dance now,'
the fairy godmother said with a smile. 'It will live in you
forever. And you'll always be welcome in the Kingdom
of Fairy Godmothers,' she continued, gently tapping
Bella's charm bracelet with the wand.

'It's time for you to go home,' she said on the last tap. 'And thank you for saving this opening night.'

All at once, the wand shrank and attached itself to the bracelet, and Bella, Roy and the mouse were gone.

Back in the attic, Dad popped his head through the door. 'I think we should leave a little bit early for the ballet try-outs. I've just heard on the radio that there are roadworks along the way.'

Bella and Roy looked up at the clock together. Then they locked eyes.

'What's wrong, you two?' Dad asked. 'You look like you've been up to something you shouldn't have. Have you?'

Bella began to giggle. 'Maybe we have,' she answered, giving Roy a pat. 'We'll be down right away.'

'I'll get the truck out of the garage then,' Dad said as he closed the door behind him.

'No time has passed since we left,' Bella chuckled to Roy once they were alone. 'How can that be?'

'And now there's no time for one last practice for your try-outs,' woofed Roy.

'Oh, I'm not worried about those,' Bella said with a wink. 'I'm going to dance Cinderella at the ball.'

'And you will do it as perfectly as you did at the Vienna State Opera House,' woofed Roy.

'It did happen, didn't it?' Bella asked as she examined the bracelet. 'And this is the Cinderella wand, isn't it? But how can that be?'

'I think it's the charm that belongs in the jewellery box drawer,' woofed Roy.

Bella looked at the wand shape cut into the foam in the small drawer. 'You're right, Roy,' she said as she pressed the wand charm into the foam.

'**It is the missing charm,**' she cried.

What Bella didn't see was another little drawer slowly beginning to open …